Blue's Garden

Published by Advance Publishers, L.C.
www.advance-publishers.com

Written by K. Emily Hutta
Art layout by J.J. Smith-Moore
Art composition by sheena needham • ess design
Produced by Bumpy Slide Books

ISBN: 1-57973-072-8

Blue's Clues Discovery Series

Blue and I are so excited! Some of the vegetables we planted in our garden are finally ready to pick and eat! Will you help us figure out which vegetables are ready to pick? You will? Great!

Hmmm. Which vegetables are ready to pick? Oh! That big head of lettuce? Yeah, it looks ready to me, too. Two cucumbers? Yep, I see them! And three bright red tomatoes! Good job! I'll bet they're nice and juicy.

So what should we do with the vegetables we just picked? Good thinking! We can use them to make lunch.

Blue, what do you think we should make for lunch? Oh! Blue wants us to play Blue's Clues to figure out what she wants to make for lunch! Terrific! I love playing Blue's Clues!

Oh! What is it, Pail?

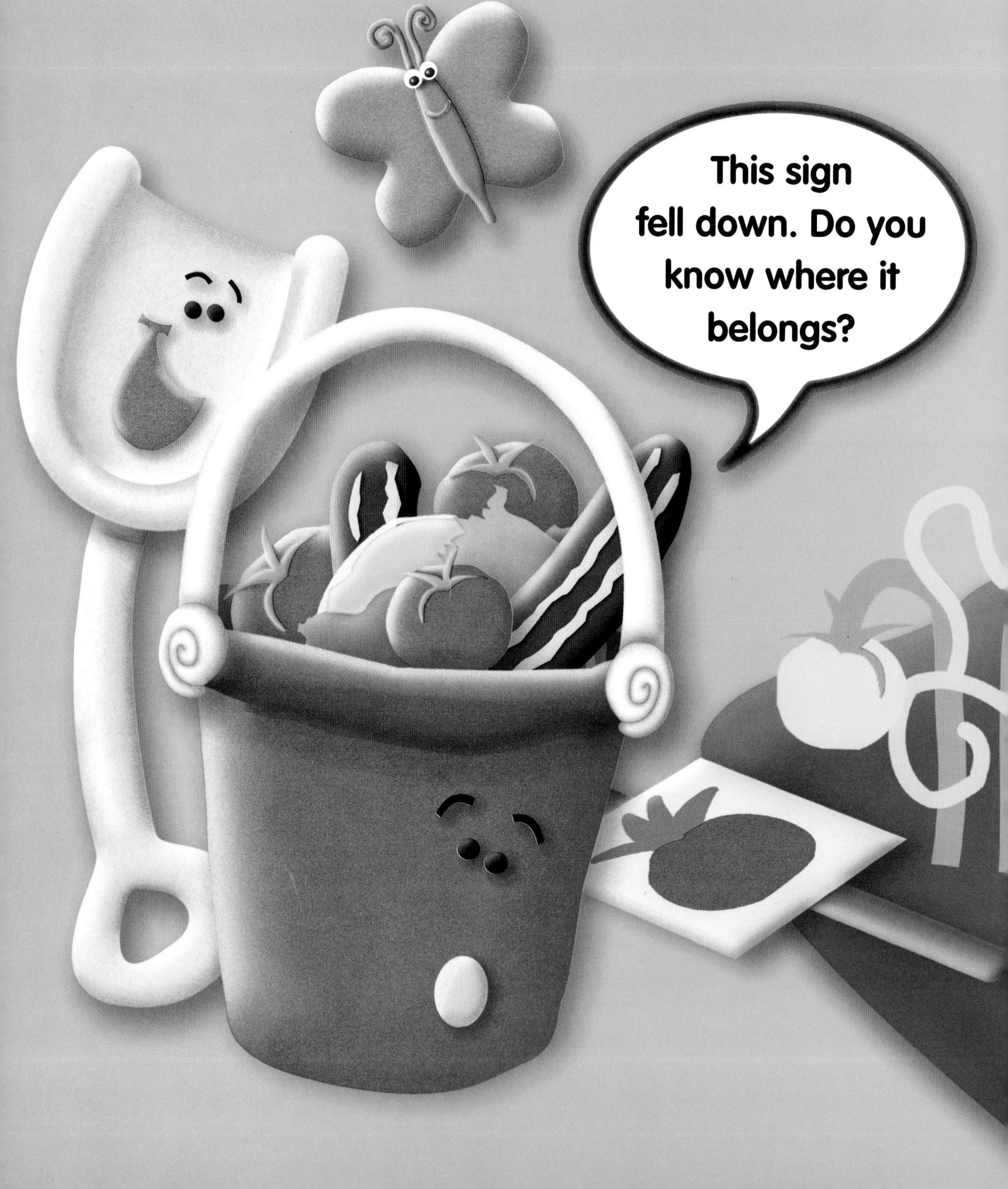

What's that a picture of? Oh! A tomato. Hey! Here's the tomato plant. But the tomato on the sign is red, and the ones on the plant are green. Right! That's because the tomato on the sign is ripe, and the ones on the plant aren't. You are so smart!

We did it! Here are the tomato plants. And now the sign is back where it belongs.

What's that? Oh, a clue! Tomatoes are our first clue! Great! But I think we need some more clues before we try and figure out the answer to Blue's Clues.

Hi, Mr. Salt and Mrs. Pepper! We just picked some vegetables from the garden. We're going to use them to make lunch. Would you like to join us?

Allo, Steve!
Allo, Blue! We would love to join you for lunch. We picked some fresh blueberries this morning. We will use them to make a pie for dessert. But first we must wash them!

Thanks for reminding me! Blue and I need to wash the vegetables we just picked, too. We'll just put the vegetables in the sink and turn on the water. A clue! You see a clue! Where? Aha! The pot! Good job!

So what does Blue want to make for lunch using tomatoes and a pot? Yeah. You're right. We should find our third clue before we try and figure out the answer.

Hi, Mailbox! You've got something for us today? Look, Blue! We sent our film away to be developed, and now we have our photos back.

I love looking at pictures!
They help me remember
things that we've done.
Thanks for the
photos, Mailbox.

Wow! Here are the pictures we took when
we planted our garden last spring!
What do you think we should
do with them? Great idea!
We'll put them on the fridge.

Oh, but the photos are all mixed up! We want to put them on the refrigerator in the same order that they happened. Will you help us? You will? Great!

What do you think happened first? Then what happened?

We did it! Our photos are all in the right order! I remember now. First we dug holes in the dirt, then we put the seeds in the holes. Then we watered the seeds, and they grew into plants. Cool!

What's that? You see a clue? Where? The soup bowl! That's our third and last clue! We have all three clues! You know what that means? It's time to go to our . . . Thinking Chair!

Now, what do you suppose Blue wants to make for lunch that uses tomatoes, a pot, and a soup bowl?

Are you thinking what I'm thinking? Something hot and tomatoey? Something like tomato soup? What do you say, Blue? Did we figure out what you want to make for lunch? We did? Hooray!